Rockets

LITTLE T

Lizard
the Wizard

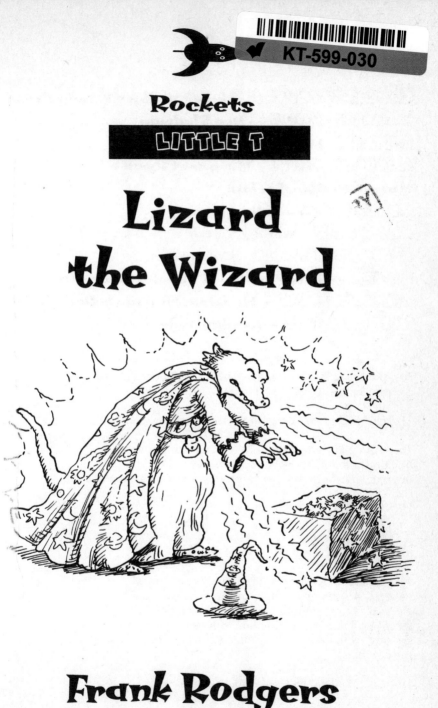

Frank Rodgers

Rockets series:

CROOK CATCHERS - Karen Wallace & Judy Brown

HAUNTED MOUSE - Dee Shulman

LITTLE T - Frank Rodgers

MOTLEY'S CREW - Margaret Ryan & Margaret Chamberlain

MR CROC - Frank Rodgers

MRS MAGIC - Wendy Smith

MY FUNNY FAMILY - Colin West

ROVER - Chris Powling & Scoular Anderson

SILLY SAUSAGE - Michaela Morgan & Dee Shulman

WIZARD'S BOY - Scoular Anderson

First paperback edition 2002
First published 2002 in hardback by A & C Black (Publishers) Ltd
37 Soho Square, London W1D 3QZ

Text and illustrations copyright © 2002 Frank Rodgers

The right of Frank Rodgers to be identified as author
and illustrator of this work has been asserted by him
in accordance with the Copyright, Designs and Patents Act 1988.

ISBN 0-7136-6048-1

A CIP catalogue record for this book is available
from the British Library.

Printed and bound by G. Z. Printek, Bilbao, Spain.

Chapter One

Little Prince T Rex was strolling through the castle. It was a sunny morning and all around him he could hear dinosaurs being happy.

His Royal Dad, King High T the Mighty, was singing in the bath.

His Royal Mum, Queen Teena Regina, was playing her trumpet for Little T's Royal Sister.

The Royal Cook was whistling merrily as he baked the morning rolls.

The Royal
Guards were
tap-dancing
up and down
instead of
marching.

Everyone is cheery this morning.

Chapter Two

But as he turned a corner Little T bumped into the Royal Magician, Lizard the Wizard.

Lizard the Wizard looked very gloomy. 'What's wrong?' asked Little T.

Everyone is happy except you!

The Royal Magician groaned.
'No wonder,' he replied. 'Every year I
have to perform a special piece of magic
to entertain the dinosaurs.'

It's called the
Magic Moment.

Cool!

'Rotten, you mean,' sighed Lizard the Wizard. 'You see, I'm not very good at Magic Moments. I get too nervous and they all turn into disasters.'

Last year I tried to magic lovely new clothes on to all of the dinosaurs.

And did you?

'Fat chance,' replied Lizard the Wizard
glumly.
'I put on my best hat, used my new
wand and tried my strongest spell.'

9

'Instead of creating new clothes...

...I made all their old clothes disappear!

There they were, all standing around in their underwear. They weren't very pleased.'

That's why they won't be looking forward to this year's Magic Moment.

Little T thought for a moment. 'I know,' he said brightly. 'Why don't you let me help you?'

I'm sure I'd be great at doing magic.

I've always wanted to be a wizard like you.

The Royal Magician looked doubtful.
'I don't know,' he said slowly.

Little T followed Lizard the Wizard to his
room.

It was full of books and bottles, cauldrons and candles, potions and powders.

'Cool!' he said, looking round. 'I really would like to be a wizard. Please,' he coaxed.

Let me try.

'I don't know...' sighed the wizard again.

Magic is not to be meddled with, you know.

'But I'm sure I can do it!' cried Little T confidently. He snatched a book from a dusty shelf. It was called *Magic Made Easy*.

I'll use this!

'But...' protested the Royal Magician.

'Don't worry,' said Little T. 'It'll be all right. I'll just read the book.'

Little T dashed off.

Chapter Three

Everyone was surprised.

Because Little T didn't just read the magic book. He tried out some of the spells.

The first ones to be surprised were his friends, Don, Bron, Tops and Dinah.

They were doing their homework.

'This homework will take ages to do,' groaned Bron.

'Forever,' said Tops.

'Don't worry,' said Little T.

This will be the fastest homework ever!

He read out a spell and...

ZOOM!

...the jotters shot out of the door.

'Oops!' gasped Little T as his friends ran after their books.

I didn't mean for the homework to go that fast!

The second ones to be surprised were the
Royal Builders. They were busy repairing
a wall.
'Phew!' said one, 'this basket of bricks is
heavy.'

'Don't worry,'
said Little T.

I'll make it
lighter!

He read out a spell.

FLASH!

'Help!' cried the Royal Builders as the basket whisked them up to the ceiling like a hot air balloon.

Oops! I didn't mean to make it so light!

The Royal Builders managed to climb down their ladders...

...then they covered the basket and nailed it to the floor until the spell wore off.

The next ones to be surprised were Little
T's mum and dad.
They were having breakfast.
The king held up his sausages.
'These are a bit small,' complained High
T the Mighty.

'Nothing I can do about it, dear,' said
Queen Teena.

'Don't worry, Dad!' called Little T.

I can make
them bigger!

He read out a spell and...

The sausages became as big as pillows
and knocked High T off his chair.

'Little T!' cried his mum. 'Take that book of spells back to the Royal Magician.'

'And don't meddle in any more magic!' spluttered his dad from underneath a giant sausage.

Chapter Four

But Little T couldn't resist one more try.
As he passed a window he looked down
into the courtyard.

The dinosaurs were there, waiting for
the Royal Magician to perform this
year's Magic Moment.

Little T had an idea.
'Don't worry,' he called.

The dinosaurs were surprised.
Because Little T's magic didn't make
their worries shrink...

FLASH!

...it made them shrink instead!

'What's going on?' they cried.
'Suddenly we're the size of mice!'

The dinosaurs' dogs and cats thought
they were mice and began to chase
them.
'Help!' cried the dinosaurs, scurrying
about in panic.

They darted this way and that, trying
not to be caught by their own pets!

Little T dashed outside.
His friends were just returning with their jotters.
'Thank goodness!' he gasped.

Quick! Help me to rescue them!

Don, Bron, Tops and Dinah dashed all over the courtyard with Little T.

They managed to pick up all the tiny dinosaurs and put them in a cardboard box.

'This is all your fault!' they squeaked at Little T in annoyance.

Change us back to normal!

Little T blushed.

'I don't know how to,' he said.

Only Lizard the Wizard can do that.

'Then go and get him!' cried the tiny dinosaurs.

QUICKLY!!

Chapter Five

Little T left Don to look after the box full
of dinosaurs...

...while he, Bron, Tops and Dinah rushed
off to look for the Royal Magician.
But Lizard the Wizard was nowhere to
be found.

He had decided to hide in case he
disgraced himself once more at the
Magic Moment.

'Where can he be?' cried Little T.
He and his friends looked everywhere.

Under Royal
Beds...

...behind Royal
Curtains...

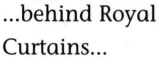

...and inside
Royal
Cupboards.

But Lizard the
Wizard seemed to
have disappeared.
Disappointed, they
went back to the
courtyard.

'I wonder if he used a vanishing spell?' murmured Little T.

It's possible.

Just then he heard a muffled sneeze in an alcove behind him.
He turned round but there was nothing there... except for a big suit of armour.

Aha!

Climbing on his friends' shoulders he reached up and lifted the visor of the helmet.

'Achoo!' sneezed Lizard the Wizard glumly.

It's dusty in here.

'You have to come out,' said Little T.

The dinosaurs need you.

No, they don't.

Yes, they do!

Quickly he told the Royal Magician what had happened.

Lizard the Wizard looked nervous.
'Oh dear,' he said.
'I suppose I will
have to help them,
won't I!'

He climbed out of the suit of armour
and followed Little T and his friends
across the courtyard.

The Royal Magician gasped when he saw what was in the cardboard box. 'Nice bit of magic,' he whispered to Little T. 'I'm impressed.'

It's better than I could do.

Little T shook his head. 'It was an accident,' he whispered back.

The tiny dinosaurs waved at Lizard the Wizard.

'Thank goodness you're here!' they squeaked.

Lizard the Wizard smiled. It was the first time the dinosaurs had ever been pleased to see him.

Suddenly he didn't feel nervous any more. He knew he mustn't let them down. This must be a perfect Magic Moment... with no mistakes.

He concentrated hard. Shutting his eyes (and crossing his fingers) he chanted a powerful spell...

FLASH!

...and suddenly the courtyard was filled with normal-sized dinosaurs again. 'You did it!' they cried in delight. 'A perfect Magic Moment!'

Hooray for Lizard the Wizard!!

Lizard the Wizard beamed
happily. At last one of his pieces
of magic had worked!
But he knew it might
not be as good the
next time.
He held up his hands.
'Dinosaurs!' he said.

I have come
to a decision.

'That was the last Magic Moment I will
ever perform. It was terrific, I agree.'

But ... 'Always
leave them wanting
more '..... that's
my motto!

Being polite, the dinosaurs pretended
they were disappointed.
'Oh, surely not,' they said.

Little T thought they meant it.

'Don't worry!' he cried. 'I've always wanted to be a wizard. You will have a Magic Moment next year!'

I'll do it!

Don, Bron, Tops and Dinah gasped.
'Oh no you won't!' they cried. 'No more magic!'
Quickly they snatched away the book of spells.

We're going to hide this!

'That's no problem,' said Little T.

'I think I remember some of the spells.'

I don't need the book.

He grinned. 'Next year's Magic Moment is going to be the best ever!'

Everyone groaned but Little T laughed. 'You just wait,' he said.